How to Be a SUPERHERO

By Sue Fliess

Illustrated by Nikki Dyson

A GOLDEN BOOK • NEW YORK

Published in the United States by Golden Books, an imprint of Random House Children's Books, a division of Random House LLC, 1745 Broadway, New York, NY 10019, and in Canada by Random House of Canada Limited, Toronto, Penguin Random House Companies. Golden Books, A Golden Book, A Little Golden Book, the G colophon, and the distinctive gold spine are registered trademarks of Random House LLC.
Visit us on the Web!
randomhouse.com/kids
Educators and librarians, for a variety of teaching tools, visit us at
RHTeachersLibrarians.com
Library of Congress Control Number: 2013946483
ISBN 978-0-385-38737-8
Printed in the United States of America
10 9 8 7 6 5 4 3 2 1
Random House Children's Books supports the First Amendment and celebrates the right to read.

GALORE
BOOKS GALORE STORE
BOOKS GALORE

"Someone help us!
Stop those crooks!
They've just stolen all our books!"

"Captain Mighty, are you near?
We could use some help down here!"

"Captain Mighty saves the day!"
MAYOR

"Never fear! I'm here to stay!"

"Will you teach me what you do?
Could I be a hero, too?"

"You can be one if you're smart
and you try with all your heart."

"Ready, Captain!"

"Come with me.
A superhero soon you'll be!

"Choose a costume:

shield or cape?

Boots to make a quick escape?

"What's your power?
Strength or
speed?

These are things all heroes need.

"Secret weapon: webs or quills?
X-ray vision?
Ninja skills?

"Force fields,

trapdoors,

stealth disguise . . .

Heroes have
to improvise!

"What's your weakness?"

"Brussels sprouts.
Make me turn my insides out!"

"Show you're fearless, brave, and tough.
Strut your superhero stuff.
Most important—grab your mask.
Now you must complete your task.
Stick with me, kid. Watch and learn. . . .
Bad guys lurk at every turn!

"Great gazookas! Turbo Troll!
He attacks with mind control!
Get your gadget! Fight his spell.
Use your super-senses well!

“Flip him!
Throw him!
Tie him down!

“Save the mayor! Save the town!

"Kid, you did it! Passed the test!
Did your superhero best!

Here's your medal! Take a bow. . . .

HUFF
MAYOR

"You're the **Silver Cyclone** now!"
WHOOSH!